About the Author

Born in 1948, Colin was the youngest of two brothers. Having a grandad who had his own farm where he spent most of his childhood, that was where he got his love for animals and the great outdoors. His father was a coal miner, as were all his uncles.

The author left school at the age of fifteen and started work at a local joiners-cum-undertakers. Colin retired from his bespoke furniture, design and making business at the age of 63. He did not start writing until the death of his beloved wife, Lesley.

Dedication

Dedicated to all grandparents who love to read or just tell stories to their grandchildren.

Colin Hirst

Ambra's Winter On The Farm

AUSTIN MACAULEY PUBLISHERS™

LONDON · CAMBRIDGE · NEW YORK · SHARJAH

A CIP catalogue record for this title is available from the British Library.

ISBN 9781398487291 (Paperback)
ISBN 9781398487307 (ePub e-book)

www.austinmacauley.com

First Published 2023
Austin Macauley Publishers Ltd
1 Canada Square
Canary Wharf
London
E14 5AA

CHAPTER ONE
THE FAMILY REUNION

Ambra and her mother both remained there motionless staring at one another, could it really be true that they had found one another after all this time? Ambra had thought her family were lost forever and her mum thought that Ambra had died the day her nest was destroyed.

It was her mum that spoke first. "How did you, what did you?" Her mum could not think clearly what to say.

Ambra said "It's a long story, Mum, a very long story."

Her mum seemed to snap out of her trance. "It's getting dark, let me get you to safety, follow me."

They both took off and started to fly away from the big house. Ambra stuck close to her mum, she wasn't going to lose her again. As they flew on it got darker and darker, then her mum called "We're here."

They started to descend and flew into an old barn. When they landed on rafters in the roof there were already four other blackbirds perched there.

Her mum said to three of them, "Meet your sister."

They all looked at Ambra in amazement. She didn't recognise her brothers, she was only seven days old when her nest had been destroyed, but she recognised her dad straight away and rush over to hug him and then hugged her mum, the tears were rolling down both their cheeks as they hugged.

Her mum said "I'll never forget that day you disappeared, I'm sure the workmen had no idea you were there when they removed the rainwater gutter and your nest tumbled down into the garden. As soon as the workmen left, we came looking for you, but what we saw made our blood run cold, that pesky cat was playing with the nest and you were nowhere to be seen, we thought the cat had eaten you, we kept calling you, but, but..." Tears appeared in her mum's eyes.

Ambra hopped over to her mum. "It's alright Mum, it's alright, I'm here now." She hugged her mum.

"Come on then Ambra, what really happened?"

CHAPTER TWO
AMBRA'S STORY

"There's so much to tell. I remember that you and Dad were feeding me, then you stopped and gave the alarm call. So, quick as a flash, I got down into the bottom of the nest, and the nest fell into a bush and sprang back up throwing me into the garden! I wasn't hurt, just a bit of a sore bum. Dad was still giving the alarm call, so I hid in the bush; I don't know how long I hid but I started to get really cold, so I hopped over to the wall. It was sunny there, that's when the cat saw me. Luckily, I could get inside the wall through a little hole before the cat could get me. I managed to get out of the wall on the other side while the cat was trying to get into the hole that I'd just entered. I crossed over the road looking for somewhere to hide, but the cat was now on the top of the wall and saw me, he sprang off the wall to come and get me, but lucky for me he nearly got run over by a car! By the time he got to my side of the road I'd found a place to hide inside a car."

"YOU HID IN A CAR!?" one of her brothers said.

"Yes, that's exactly what I did," Ambra replied.

"WOW, I've never been in a car," the same brother remarked.

"Stop interrupting," Dad said, staring at his son.

"That's when things got really scary," Ambra continued. "From my hiding place in the car I could see the road surface, I could also see the cat, he was mystified as to where I had gone, but then someone got into the car and the cat scarpered. If I had known what was about to happen I would have scarpered as well. There was a click and then an almighty noise as the car started to move, the road surface below me became just a blur as we went faster and faster. Before the car had set off I was feeling really chilly but now it was nice and warm, then it became much too warm, then it got really hot. The metal plate I was standing on became so hot I had to stand on one foot then the other foot, now my feet were burning. I was hopping and hopping but the plate was too hot to stand on. The car came to a stop and I immediately jumped down onto the road. Lucky for me there was a puddle at the side of the road; I jumped into it with both feet, it was bliss standing there in that puddle. After a moment I realised that now I must be miles from home and would probably never see any of you again."

Ambra stayed quiet for quite a while, then her mum said "Are you okay to carry on?"

Ambra regathered herself, "Right, okay," she said, "on we go. I looked around in all directions and decided to go down the embankment at my side of the road, towards the woods. I came to a small stream and found a fallen log that I could cross the stream on, I had only just crossed over when I spied a lovely big fat worm, and I was starving so I started to eat it, but no sooner had I started to eat it, when it was snatched away by a great big spiny monster that was standing right in front of me." There was a gasp from all the family. "It wasn't really a monster, it was a hedgehog named Doug who was really friendly and he look after me, he saved my life and became my best friend."

Mum said she thought that was enough for one day, "Maybe Ambra will tell us more about Doug tomorrow, it's time to get some sleep."

Ambra hadn't realised how tired she was, before she knew it she awoke and it was already morning, she looked for any of her family but saw no one. She started to think it had all been a dream about meeting her mum, then her mum's voice came from behind her. "Good morning sleepy head. I didn't want to wake you, you were sound asleep."

CHAPTER THREE
AMBRA'S NEW HOME

Ambra could now see the full size of the barn and it was gigantic. Below her she saw lots of different farm vehicles all parked in rows; to the left side of the barn straw bales were stacked twenty bales high, to the right the same amount of hay bales were stacked, there were sacks of all shapes and sizes all stacked in neat piles.

Mum said "Come on, I'll show you round the area."

So off they went, the area around the barn was all new to Ambra, there were fields, heathland, forests, and a large pond with marsh land to one side. Ambra suddenly realised she was starving. Yesterday she hadn't felt like eating but now she needed food.

Ambra's mum seemed to have sensed Ambra's hunger. "Let's get some food," she said.

After they had eaten they flew high into a tree and rested to let their food digest. As Ambra looked around her new surroundings she could not remember which way they had come from last night; she was frightened that if she could not find the big house she would not be able to find Doug.

"Mum, how do I get back to the big house?"

"We'll have a rest and I'll show you," her mum replied.

Over the next few weeks Ambra settled into the daily routine of the farm. Five people lived on the farm; the farmer, his wife and two children, a boy and a girl, there was also an older man who milked the cows. They also had two dogs: a Jack Russell called Lady and a sheep dog called Jess.

Twice a day the cows came in for milking, the farmer came into the barn in his tractor for hay every morning, he came for straw once a week, the hay was for the cows to eat and the straw was for bedding. The farmer's wife came every morning with a wheelbarrow for a sack of cattle nuts; Lady the Jack Russell was always with her. After the cows had been milked, the hens were let out of the hen shed along with the ducks and geese, then the eggs collected. Work on the farm never seemed to stop.

Sometimes Ambra went off with her mum, sometimes she went on her own. Once when she was alone, she came upon a place she knew well, she had often been there with Doug. Doug was her best friend, she knew Doug far better than she knew her family, she thought of him as her father, for it was he who had brought her up. She flew to the cliff where she'd learnt to fly. Below her she knew that in a small cave at the base of the cliff Doug would be fast asleep and that he would sleep all winter, because that's what hedgehogs do.

When she returned to the barn that evening all the family were there, she had seen her eldest brother swoop into the barn just before her. They all talked about their day and what they had seen and done.

Before going to sleep one of her brothers said, "Tell us about when you and Doug got washed down the river."

"No, tells us about your car journey."

"NO NO, tells us about when Doug fell into the hole."

Over the last few weeks she had told all these stories about her adventures with Doug many times, her brothers never tired of the stories.

The hours of daylight had become really short and some days it didn't seem to get light at all, and the last two days had been really cold; it was so cold at night that all the family snuggled together to keep warm.

The next morning when Ambra went to the pond for a drink, she was amazed the water was no longer a liquid but solid, that's when she remembered that Doug had once told her about water turning to something like stone when the weather became really cold. She had to fly to the water trough in the cattle shed to drink.

All that day the weather got a lot worse, the wind had become so strong it was hard to fly, it wasn't rain that fell but hailstones. The whole family returned early to the safety of the barn.

CHAPTER FOUR
WINTER ARRIVES

The next morning the wind had dropped, Ambra's eldest brother was the first to leave the barn but return straightaway.

"Everyone, come and see this," he said.

They all followed him outside. What they saw was a world transformed; it was completely white. Half a metre of snow covered the land, the buildings, the trees, even the pond was covered.

Dad said "I've seen snow before, but nothing like this."

They all landed together on the pristine snow, their feet sank into the soft snow making it hard to walk. Ambra was fascinated by her tracks in the snow, perfect footprints followed her everywhere she went. It wasn't long before her brothers started flicking snow at one another, Ambra could not resist joining in, the snow was flying everywhere, it was like a snowstorm, they were laughing and chirping and generally being silly. Then one of her brothers decided to make an impression of himself in the snow. He spread his wings deep into the snow, then pushed down his tail, next he pushed his head down, and he jumped up leaving a perfect impression of a bird in flight. They all tried making their own impressions, then argued about whose was best.

Dad announced "It will have to be berries for breakfast." He took off from the snow and they all followed. He took them to the edge of the woods where three rowan trees stood, they were bright red with berries.

When they had eaten their fill Dad said to Ambra "I'll show you another tree that is good for berries."

She followed him further into the woods, once again she saw the red berries before they arrived at the tree, this was a holly tree.

On landing in the tree her father said "These other mottled birds are field fairs, they're on their way south."

The other birds were slightly bigger than Ambra, they looked a bit like thrushes. Ambra said "Hello" to the bird nearest to her.

"Eeloo, me am Ivor, I have corn froom Russia."

"My name is Ambra, is it very far from Russia?"

"Yar, many days we fly too geet here, I reest and feed then go further sooth."

"WOW," said Ambra.

She asked her dad why the other birds were going south. Her dad explained, "Lots of birds fly south for winter, where they live in summer it's warm, but in winter it gets ten times colder than here, far too cold to survive, so the further south you go the warmer it gets, and when the summer returns to the north they fly all the way back."

"I'm glad I live here," she said.

"Me too," her dad said.

When they returned to the farm after breakfast the cows had already been milked, and the ducks and geese were out but the hens remained in the shed. The farmer was busy moving the snow from the yard; he had attached something to the front of the tractor and he was pushing the snow to one side of the yard.

The older man who milked the cows was busy attaching something to the other tractor, Ambra wondered if he was the grandad to the children? This tractor was far bigger than the other one, it had enormous wheels, and it now had something like a crate attached to the back of it. The man threw a large shovel and a long thin stick into the back, he climbed into the cab of the tractor; a puff of black smoke came from the rear of the tractor as he drove out of the barn. He stopped briefly next to the other tractor, spoke to the farmer, then continued out of the yard into the field making deep tracks in the snow.

Ambra flew back into the barn and watched in fascination as the farmer's wife and the children were making an enclosure with straw bales. The boy was pushing straw bales from the top of the stack down to his mum who was making the bales into walls three bales high. The girl was sliding the bales into place to create the shape of the enclosure, she wasn't yet strong enough to lift the bales, so Mum put the top two layers on. The enclosure was now finished but it lacked a gate.

Ambra heard the big tractor approaching, it reversed up to the enclosure, lowered the crate and the man climbed down from the tractor cab and opened the door to the crate, out came about ten sheep. He and the farmer's wife went down the side of the barn and returned with a metal gate, while Jess the sheep dog made sure the sheep stayed put while the gate was fitted. They stood the gate across the entrance to the enclosure, and after moving some more bales of straw the gate could slide back and forth.

Meanwhile, outside the farmer had cleared the snow from the yard and the track right up to where it met the road, he now entered the barn and spoke to his family. He then got another shovel, threw it into the crate and Jess the sheep dog jumped into the back, the driver got back into the cab followed by the farmer and his son and off they went.

Back in the barn the farmer's wife was dragging a metal trough to the enclosure, the girl was dragging a hosepipe behind her. Once the trough was placed inside the enclosure the girl put the hose into the trough and then disappeared outside, soon water was flowing into the trough and the sheep ran across to drink. Meanwhile, Mum was shaking hay bales apart for the sheep to eat.

CHAPTER FIVE
THE GREAT RESCUE

Two of Ambra's brothers flew in, they were really excited. "Come see this!" they shouted and flew out again. Mum, Dad and Ambra flew after them.

They followed the deep tracks in the snow to where the farmer was digging the deep snow away from a wall that had been completely covered with the snow. Further down the wall there was already a large hole in the snow, the other man was walking on the top of the wall poking the long stick down into the snow, moving on and sticking the pole repeatedly down through the snow, then once he located a sheep under the snow, he jumped off the wall into the snow and started to dig. The farmer had dug out the snow to the bottom of the wall and was pulling out a sheep, he checked the sheep over then placed it into the crate, then another. One of the sheep wasn't moving when it was dragged out of the snow, the farmer was checking the mouth and nose of the sheep, then he turned it over and started rubbing and squashing its chest, the sheep coughed and gasped; it was alive, the farmer lifted the sheep into the crate and went back to get more sheep out of the snow. The crate was now full, but the farmer kept on digging out sheep, telling Jess to keep them where they were.

Ambra's brothers were shouting again and pointing towards the road; they all flew off towards the road. A large yellow lorry with orange flashing lights was pushing the snow off the road. The lorry was going quite fast and snow was flying right over the roadside wall; as it passed it was spinning something out of the back onto the road surface.

By midday more and more sheep were arriving at the barn and the farmer's wife appeared carrying a tray and the little girl was carrying a metal cylinder. The tray was placed on some bales that were pushed to one side. When the latest batch of sheep were safe in the barn they all went and sat on the bales next to the tray, they all took wipes from a container on the tray and wiped their hands. Then the cover over the tray was lifted off to reveal mugs, sandwiches, pies and cakes; hot drinks were poured from the cylinder causing steam to rise into the air. The farmer's wife gave the children a bottle of water each, in no time at all the tray was empty.

After the break, the men went back to dig more sheep out of the snow, the farmer's wife and the girl took the tray back to the house and the boy went to the hen house to start collecting the eggs. His mum and his sister came to help collect eggs as well and while his mum and sister carried the trays of eggs back to the house the boy went to get the ducks and geese back into the shed; all he had to do was rattle a bucket of food and they all raced back to the shed, then the boy went back to the house.

The big yellow lorry with the orange flashing lights came back the other way, now both sides of the road were clear of snow.

The man who looked after the cows had to stop digging snow so he could milk the cows again. Once they were milked, he went back to digging the sheep out of the snow. The daylight was now fading, it would be soon dark and Ambra's mum flew up to perch next to her.

She had been for a drink of water from the water trough and heard the sheep talking, "Two sheep are still missing," she told Ambra, "it will be too dark soon to continue the search," she said.

Outside, the farmer was about to give up the search, he didn't want to leave two sheep in the snow all night, they would not survive another night, but they couldn't move all the snow, then he heard Jess the sheep dog barking. They rushed over to see what all the fuss was about, she was jumping into a hole sniffing then jumping back out and trying to dig another hole.

The farmer rushed to get both shovels, both men began to dig, it wasn't long before both men were pulling out sheep. They had one each, and they put them into the crate. The farmer went over to Jess and gave her vigorous rub, saying "Good girl, good girl."

They put the shovels and long stick into the crate and the farmer lifted Jess up into the cab and they both joined her, the other man started the tractor and they set off back home.

When they arrived back in the barn and both sheep placed into the enclosure, the whole family came together and high fived one another, laughed and had a group hug, even Jess and Lady got a fuss made of them.

It was now dark outside, but then headlights illuminated the yard; it was the milk lorry that had come to collect today's milk. The farmer said to the driver "Glad you could make it."

"What a day," the driver said.

"Yes, what a day," the farmer said, the whole family laughed. "Just another day on the farm," he said.

A few minutes after the milk lorry had left with his milk the lights in the barn were switched off and darkness ensued.

CHAPTER SIX
EVERYTHING IS CALM

Dad was telling her brothers to stop being silly, she couldn't see what they were up to but there was lots of giggling going on.

"Dad," Ambra said, "why did the sheep let themselves get buried, why didn't they just move?"

"I think that with the strong cold wind they just got down to sleep next to the wall to get out of the wind, when it started to snow, they probably thought it would soon stop, but the snow came so fast and so heavy that they didn't have time to move before they got trapped," Dad replied.

Then Mum said "They were very lucky the farmer knew where to look and knew how to get them out." They all agreed on that.

The next day was a lot calmer, the cows were milked and fed, the sheep fed and watered, hens fed and eggs collected, the geese and duck let out, but the hens remained inside, and the children went off to school.

Ambra flew to the holly tree; she was alone, the fieldfares must have continued on their journey. After she had eaten, she decided to go to the big house to see what food had been left out for the other animals.

Once there she perched in a nearby tree to see what sort of animals came to feed. First were the squirrels, they were picking peanuts off the ground, eating some and hiding others. A female badger arrived which scared the squirrels away; she began to eat peanuts, she then went to check the dishes at the back door; she had a drink of water.

Ambra knew that the food that Doug enjoyed would not be put out until evening, badgers normally didn't come out of their setts until after dark, it must have been the extreme weather and hunger that had forced her out in the daylight. She also saw a few mice under the bird table, an assortment of birds were on the feeders. She continued to watch a bit longer; secretly she was hoping to see a hedgehog, but none came. She returned to the barn.

CHAPTER SEVEN
THE BIG MELT

After five days of freezing temperatures the weather finally began to warm up, water began to pour off the roofs and the pond appeared again. After three days the only snow left was up against the wall where the sheep had been buried. The next day the sheep were returned to the fields and the barn was quiet again. Ambra and her family decided to have a change from eating berries and set off to find worms, bugs or anything else that took their fancy.

A few days later one of Ambra's brothers came looking for her. "Come on, the farmer has just connected the plough to the tractor." She didn't understand what all the fuss was about but followed her brother.

They joined the rest of the family just as the tractor arrived at the field.

"What's all the fuss about?" she asked.

"Just wait and see," her mum replied.

As soon as the plough was lowered to the ground the excitement in the family rose. The farmer began to plough the field; as the plough moved forward the corn stubble was turned right over and was now under the ground and bare soil had turned to the top exposing all the worms and invertebrates. Ambra now saw what all the fuss had been about, and she joined the rest of the family feasting on all the food the plough had exposed.

When she could not eat any more, she flew across the field and landed in the boundary hedge. Perched deep in the hedge she decided to have a snooze.

She was dozing away when she heard someone call "Help!"

She stirred a little, *I must be dreaming*, she thought and started to doze again.

"HELP HELP!" There was no mistaking this latest cry for help, she was fully awake now and listened carefully for any further noises.

There was a rustling and scraping noise down below and off to one side; off she went to investigate. To her amazement, there just in front of her was a young badger struggling to free herself from the sheep netting that had been put in place to block a gap in the hedge.

As soon as she saw Ambra the young badger started to cry. "I can't get free," she said.

"Let me have a look," Ambra replied. She checked all around the badger, but the situation didn't look good. The badger had got her head and one leg through the mesh of the netting and now she could neither go forward nor backwards.

Ambra tried to comfort the young badger by asking what her name was.

"Kirra," she replied.

"Okay, Kirra, I am going to get you out of there." She had no idea how, but she didn't mention that to the young badger. "Where are your mum or dad, do you know?"

"I was with Mum last night but lost sight of her; I waited a while but when she didn't return I tried to find my own way home, that's when I got stuck."

"I'm going to find your mum, just stay calm until I get back." Ambra flew off and landed out of sight of the badger; there was no point going to find the young badger's mum, her mum couldn't free her daughter, *it's all down to me to come up with a plan*, she thought.

CHAPTER EIGHT
AMBRA'S ESCAPE PLAN

Perched high in a tree looking out over the field, Ambra watched the farmer going backwards and forwards ploughing the field; every time he finished a row and turned the tractor, he got a bit closer to her. She was thinking how the farmer had rescued the sheep, could he maybe rescue the badger? How could she get the farmer's attention was her next thought, she didn't know but she had to try.

She left her perch and set off for the tractor, she landed on the bonnet of the tractor, hopped up to the windscreen and started to tap with her beak, TAP, TAP, TAP, TAP, then she flew up and down the windscreen flapping her wings, then she flew off in the direction of the badger. The farmer watched in disbelief, what was wrong with that crazy bird?

Soon Ambra was back on the tractor TAP, TAP, TAP, TAP then fluttered up and down the windscreen, and then off again in the direction of the badger. The farmer kept ploughing, but Ambra did not give up, backwards and forward TAP, TAP,TAP,TAP, and every time flying back towards the badger; she had lost count of how my times she had tapped on the tractor, but finally the farmer realised that this crazy bird was trying to tell him something. He also noticed that she always flew back to the same spot, maybe he should go have a look.

When he got to the end of the row he lifted the plough out of the ground, and set off for the spot where the crazy bird had always returned.

Meanwhile, back at the fence Ambra was thinking it was time to go back to tractor, but she noticed the farmer had stopped his ploughing and was heading her way; *it was working!* she thought.

The tractor was now coming down the side of the field with its plough in the air. As it approached her Ambra once again started to fly straight up and down in the air at the exact spot where the badger was trapped. The tractor stopped and the engine switched off, the farmer got down from the tractor and walk straight towards Ambra, at the same time as the farmer arrived Ambra flew down and landed on the badger.

"It's me, Kirra, I've got some help, just stay calm."

At the same time farmer said to himself "Now then, crazy bird, what's all the fuss about?" It didn't take him long to see the badger, he bent down and had a closer look, but then he returned to the tractor.

Ambra could not believe that he was leaving, but when the farmer got back to the tractor he opened a small door in the side of the tractor and removed a box and walked back to the badger with it.

He opened the box and removed something and bent down next to the badger. Ambra could not see what he was doing but she heard, snip, snip, snip, then all at once Kirra was free. She shot off into the woods without a backward glance.

After a few more snips the farmer stood and looked straight at Ambra, he put out his hand, tickled her chest, nodded at her and went on his way. He could not wait to tell his family what had happened, never in his life had he known of such a thing.

Ambra hopped down to see how the farmer had managed to free Kirra, there was now a hole in the wire fence big enough to let any other badgers pass through safely.

CHAPTER NINE
AMBRA MEETS THE MAJOR

On her way back to the barn Ambra decided to go to the pond for a drink. Landing at the edge of the pond, she had not noticed that there was a toad just to one side of her; it was so well camouflaged that it was only when it moved did she become aware of it.

"Sorry, I didn't mean to startle you, I'm the Major," the toad said.

"Oh hello, I'm Ambra, it's nice to meet you, Major, do you live in the pond?" she asked.

"No, no, no, toads don't live in ponds, we only come to the pond to mate," he said.

"Oh, I didn't know that," Ambra responded.

"I live in the undergrowth of the fields and the forest, I'm only here to find a lady friend you see."

"Oh." Ambra didn't quite know what to say.

"Yes, yes, once I've found her and fertilised her eggs, I'm back to the fields; I've better things to do than dawdle about here."

"Oh," Ambra muttered.

"Ha, there's a female over there, see you," and with one enormous leap into the pond, he was gone. Ambra was sure her beak had turned red, she felt quite embarrassed by the Major's candid remarks.

That evening when her mum asked her what sort of day she'd had, she told her mum about the farmer's rescue of the badger, but she didn't mention her part in the rescue, she was just happy that Kirra was free.

"I also got talking to a toad called the Major."

"Ah, you've met the Major have you," and laughed, "he's quite a character!" Ambra was sure her beak had gone red again.

"Mum, don't male toads help to look after their babies?"

Her mum told her that not even their mum would stay to look after them.

"Wow," Ambra said.

Her mum went on to tell her, "The eggs don't hatch into toads, but into tadpoles and only later did they change into toads. Frogs do the same thing, and are left completely on their own, and have to survive the best way they can."

"WOW," Ambra said again, "that's tough."

"You managed on your own," her mother said with a sad look on her face.

Ambra gave her mum a cuddle. "No way would I have survived without Doug," was Ambra's reply.

"You really miss him, don't you?"

I've got all my family back and that's wonderful, but yes, I do miss him." It was her mum's turn to hug Ambra now.

CHAPTER TEN
HER BROTHERS DECIDED ON A PRANK

Ambra had noticed her brothers in a huddle making plans, and now they were busy collecting stones and placing them on a beam in the barn; she decided to see what they were up to.

"Come on, let me in on your secret," she said.

"It's no secret," they replied, "we are going to get our own back on Lady."

If Lady ever saw them on the ground she would run and chase them off barking as she did so. They explained they were going to gather lots of stones and then tempt Lady right underneath them and then bombard her with stones. This sounded like good fun to Ambra, she too had been chased by Lady many times. It was amazing to see the size of some of the stones her eldest brother could carry, but really they were still only small pebbles, but it still took great strength to carry a pebble.

Everything was set, all they had to do was wait until Lady appeared.

It seemed to take ages before she came sniffing around. It had been decided that the youngest brother would try and get Lady right underneath them; a pebble had been placed on the exact spot on the ground.

As soon as Lady saw a bird on the floor in her barn she was off giving chase, but when she stopped her chase she wasn't quite in the right spot. She was just a tiny bit short of the mark, so when Lady started to retreat out of the barn the younger brother flew back down to the barn floor just a bit closer than last time, but Lady hadn't noticed him, so he started to chirp.

It worked, Lady gave chase again, this time when she stopped, she was right next to the marker pebble.

"NOW!" her brothers shouted.

With their feet they all started to shower stones down onto Lady; poor Lady could not understand what was happening, it was raining stones!

She ran back to the house yelping, she was making so much noise, the farmer's wife came out to see what was happening, but Lady shot straight past her into the house. The farmer's wife could see no one about so she went back into the house herself.

"Great plan," they all said and rolled about in fits of laughter.

It didn't have any long-term effect on Lady, she was soon back chasing them, but now they just smiled to themselves when they flew away. Their mum and dad never did find out what all the laughter was about that evening.

CHAPTER ELEVEN
THE SHEEP ARE BACK

They were all curious when a large lorry reversed into the barn. When it stopped, two men got out of the cab, and they began to unload lots of metal fence panels. The farmer, his wife, and the older man came into the barn and started to help unloading the lorry, the children were at school, so not around to join in.

Once the lorry had been unloaded the driver climbed into the cab and moved the lorry to just outside the door to the barn. He returned to join the others, they began to erect the fence panels in what looked to be a well-practiced maneuver; two hours later the job was done.

They looked down at a vast area of different sized pens made out of the fence panels; some pens were ten panels square, the smallest only one panel square. As soon as the job was finished the two men returned to the lorry and left, the others returned to their own chores.

So Ambra and her family all decided to leave the barn themselves; Ambra thought she would go once again to see if there was any sign of her friend Doug.

She landed in a tree where she could see the entrance of the small cave where Doug was sleeping. She could see no signs of any disturbance, so after a while she decided to get something to eat.

The next morning, they were woken from their slumbers as the sheep were brought into the new pens that had been erected yesterday. Jess was making sure there were no escapees, then all the water troughs were filled and new straw bedding installed.

Before the end of the day, three of the sheep had given birth to their lambs; Ambra could see three sets of twins. All that week, day and night lambs were being born, the farmer or his wife kept a watch over the sheep even right through the night, Ambra and all her family thought it was fantastic to witness all this new life.

Some of the lambs needed to be bottle fed, and each day before school the farmer's children came armed with lots of bottles filled with milk and fed the ones that needed to be fed; sometimes two at a time. Ambra could tell this was a job they really enjoyed. Ambra was sure that there were over one hundred lambs now in the barn.

Ten days later the sheep and their lambs were taken back to the fields, just a few adult sheep and their lambs remained in the barn along with all the lambs that required to be bottle fed.

CHAPTER TWELVE
WHAT IS WRONG WITH JESS?

Ambra's mum was asking all the family when they had last seen Jess. The sheep dog hadn't been seen by anyone for at least two days, maybe even longer. Her dad remembered that Jess wasn't there when all the sheep went back to the fields and that was two days ago; that was unusual, she was always there when the sheep were being moved.

One of Ambra's brothers said that he had seen all the farmer's family leaving the hut where Jess lived early that morning before they started work and before the children went to school.

"I hope she's not ill," Ambra said.

"Someone should go and check on her," Ambra's mum said.

"I'll go," Dad said, and flew off.

After what seemed like ages Dad returned; everybody was waiting to hear what the problem with Jess was.

"Come on, come on, tell us, is it bad news?" Ambra said.

"Well, she won't be herding sheep any time soon, you better come see."

They all followed on behind, they all landed on the top of the bars on the hut and peered down at Jess; she was fast asleep, but snuggled up to her were five little black and white puppies.

"Does that answer your question?" Dad said.

Everybody laughed with joy and agreed that Jess had a fantastic new family. Everyone flew off feeling really happy; *what a great way to start the day* Ambra thought to herself.

CHAPTER THIRTEEN
DOUG AWAKES

After the fantastic sight of seeing Jess with her puppies, Ambra wondered if it could be her lucky day and find Doug awake, but when she arrived at the cliff she was disappointed that there was no sign of Doug. When Doug had entered the cave to hibernate he had told Ambra that when he had finished his hibernation he would drag some of his bedding out of the cave and leave it in a pile just outside the cave entrance, so she would know he was awake. But there was no pile of bedding; Ambra flew off and told herself to try again later.

The days were getting longer, and the temperature was getting warmer. Plants were starting to send out new shoots, trees and bushes were also showing signs of life, *so surely it couldn't be too long before Doug was awake*, she thought to herself.

But later that day and the following day there was still no sign of Doug.

That night one of Ambra's brothers told her he had seen a hedgehog in the woods over the other side of the top field. Dad also reported he had also seen one, but when he had asked its name it was Brian, not Doug.

Maybe tomorrow, she thought to herself, but at midday the next day there was still no pile of bedding. Ambra was beginning to worry that something could be wrong with Doug because now there had been quite a few sightings of hedgehogs, but her mum reassured her that he would be fine and that who was to know what tomorrow would bring.

It was mid-morning when Ambra set off to check on Doug again. As soon as she landed she was filled with joy; Doug was fine. There at the base of the cliff was a pile of bedding. There was no sign of Doug, surely it wouldn't take long to find him.

She visited some of their favourite spots, but it wasn't until she went to the stream that she heard him. She had landed in a tree near the stream but saw no one and was wondering where to go next, when she heard a familiar sound; SZZZ, SZZZ, SZZZ. It was Doug, he was fast asleep snoring.

She could not believe it; he had been asleep all winter and now he was taking a nap! That was her Doug alright, he was curled up under some brambles. She hoped he was dreaming of her, she would just wait until he woke up. She was enjoying the familiar sound and she could wait a little longer.

She didn't have long to wait. Doug stood up, gave himself an almighty shake and emerged from under the brambles.

She flew down to his side and said "Hello you," and snuggled up to his snout, "I've missed you," she said.

"It seems only like yesterday that I last saw you," Doug replied. It had never occurred to Ambra that for Doug it was just like waking up the next day! "I'm starving, what about you?"

That's my Doug, Ambra thought and laughed out loud.

"You will not believe what happened to me the day after you hibernated!" she said as they walked along together.

THE END